THE HEALER

By

Becca St. John

This is an introduction to a society of women healers,
The Women of the Woods,
and prequel to The Protector ~

An apprentice healer risks her life to save a fledgling knight ~

His brother's murdered, his father poisoned, Roland Montgomery is
left for dead in a field beneath the healer's caves.

Young Veri finds the wounded fledgling knight. In saving his life she
must abandoned her life as a healer and face the elusive danger
haunting the Montgomery family.

The Healer©2013Martha E Ferris
All rights reserved

Cover Art © 2012 Kelli Ann Morgan / Inspire Creative
Services
www.inspirecreativeservcies.com

Becky R. Long and Dr. John S. Long
Through trials and tribulations you offered a rich, diverse, history.
I love and miss you both.

Table of Contents

CHAPTER 1　~
IN THE YEAR OF OUR LORD 1214

Usnea stepped away from the sour steam, raised a beefy arm to catch rivulets of sweat dripping down her face. For a moment, she rested and assessed the other women in the clearing.

The cold damp of autumn stole the joy of sleeping, living, outdoors. Time to move from the clearing to the caves inside the mountain. They should be moved by the morrow, at the latest, although Usnea would be happy for some cold damp. She cocked an eye toward her current chore.

"Are we wishes?"

"What?" The stir paddle slipped from Usnea's hand, to bob and spin in the bubbling cauldron. Exasperated, the old woman looked about the clearing for something to catch the paddle. "Are we what?"

"Wishes. Are we wishes, like the children in the village say?"

"Ah." Usnea grabbed a shepherd's crook that lay against a boulder near the mouth of the caves. Leaning into the hot steam, she hooked the stirrer as it bumped and thumped around the wide mouth of the cauldron.

Huffing and puffing, but paddle under control, she turned away from the stench of roiling liquid and looked up to the child's favorite refuge, nestled in the crook of the old oak. A canopy of yellow and amber foliage kept her hidden.

After the night they'd all had, tending to Old Lady Thompson in the village, the child should be sleeping. She'd been freed of chores for that very reason.

"Are we?"

So easy, yet so hard to answer.

Again, Usnea glanced to the others in the clearing, the women in the woods, the healers, all too busy to help her answer the young one.

She studied the tree, the hint of leg. "Yes, child, I suppose we are wishes."

"I knew it!" Veri's brown eyes lit with success.

Veri peered through the foliage, and in that moment Usnea realized how much the child had changed over the summer. Not yet of womanhood but in her last years as a child. Her cheekbones and jaw, now more prominent, alluded to the sweetness of her nature with a face shaped like a heart.

"Aye," Usnea worked her stirrer into a rhythm, "we are wishes as the villagers would be."

Those large eyes narrowed. "No," the lass reasoned, "If they were wishes, they'd not call us such."

"True, child, true." Ignoring the boiling blankets, Usnea pulled the paddle from the cauldron. "Only, 'wishes' is not what the villagers call us."

"They do." Veri argued, hiding among the leaves once again. "I heard them, just today, when we returned from tending old lady Thompson."

"Witches," Usnea sighed, sorry for the truth of it. "It's witches they call us.

Veri swung upside down from her perch. A thick, tawny wall of hair nearly reached the ground. "Witches? What are witches?"

The older woman plopped down on a stump, the burden of reality twining with fatigue from the long night. "I couldn't tell you for a surety, sweet one, for I've never met a witch."

"But you know about them."

"Aye, from the villagers." She swiped the sweat off her brow, pushing damp tendrils of grey from her forehead. "They say witches are women with magical powers who can cast spells to make a person ill, and command the sky to do their bidding."

"Impossible!" Veri insisted.

"Hmph." Usnea shrugged. Something to think about. Possible, impossible, who is to know the difference?

Veri climbed back, legs straddling the branch. "That means we are magical."

"Hoe!" Usnea tisked impatiently. "Magical?" She murmured. "Have we not spoken of this, and often?"

Obviously, this was not answer enough for the child. Veri knew of magic and mystery, for it was in the bud of a flower, in the power of a root. She was well aware of the transfer of feeling at the birth of a babe, be it animal or human, but she knew nothing of her own mystery. That was the magic the villagers whispered about. That was the mystery that had them all making the sign of the cross whenever Veri or her "sisters" drew near. It was the element that was said to make them great healers.

"Veri," the elder commanded, "watch as I spin this thread." Usnea reached into the pocket of her dress and pulled out a simple spindle. With a flick, she dangled the spindle, spinning the finest of thread, far finer than any Veri had ever seen on any spindle but Usnea's.

"See how delicate this yarn is and yet how strong?" She stopped spinning and twanged the results of her twisting and pulling. Then, with a sideways glance at Veri, she asked, "Is it magic that I can spin such a thread?"

"The spider spins finer," Veri responded without insult.

"You are full of cheek child," Usnea laughed. "but you speak of things as they are. This is good. The spider does cast a finer thread, and is his thread made of magic?"

Hovering upon her branch, upon her answer, the child played with her thoughts. She had been taught to study all creatures, even spiders. Usnea had seen her sit in silence for hours to watch and wonder, and understand. Understanding did not offer the fun and adventure of the spirits and goblins and wee fairies of the villagers. They had fantastical religions spouting of God and Satan and whispering of other forces.

However, those thoughts, those beliefs, were not what held the Healers. They would not be swayed by mere stories of the world, they would look at it, learn, trust in reason and common sense. Because of this, Veri knew she would not be hearing what it was she wanted to hear. She would not be hearing that she was special, unique, one of those fantastical spirits.

On a sigh far too weighty for youth, she returned. "It is not magic but spittle from its body."

"Spittle it created?"

"Yes."

"And who created the spider?"

Veri slumped upon her perch. So many of her questions ended upon the same answer. It was the magic of life once more. One is not magical, life is magical. Creation is magical. Not one body but the flow of one body into another. This meant she was no different than the village children. She was not magical at all. She was not special or unique.

Usnea knew, all too well, it made the ostracism more painful.

The sound of horses pulled the old woman's attention to a path that led into the trees.

One motion, a command, and she knew the child would pull back within the shelter of the foliage. A quick glance proved more signals, sent from others in the clearing, stilled the girl from questions that billowed. Silenced, she would remain steady and quiet in her nest of leaves.

Horses that jangled with silver dressings were ominous indeed. Those who owned horses rarely came this way. Those who could costume them in fine metal never came. They might send their servants, demand the women go to them, but never, ever, had the powerful ones come to the caves.

In a rush and swirl of glinting armor, riders broke into camp. The mass of horse and men swallowed up the work yard. Attendant peasants, on foot, brandished tools as weapons, swarmed through the camp.

In the thick of it all was the priest.

Father Ignacious.

He wore no armor, other than the cape of office. He rode no war-seasoned horse but a finer-boned stallion of less controllable ilk. The villagers feared this man and his dark, beady eyes that flared with madness. He had a long, angular face, exaggerated by a beard clipped to an arrow's point. It was a gaunt and sinister design.

The high-strung horse danced about, confused by all the activity. He knocked Tansy over, as if she were of no more importance than a troublesome gnat. Veri sickened as she fought the urge to jump down, to run to Tansy's side. But she had been silenced, given the signal of learning. She was to watch and see, to be invisible and understand.

Tansy, in her gown of reed, lay on the ground, her crown of tansy flowers scattered about her head making her look more foolish than gifted. This woman of wisdom and soul should be treated with respect and reverence, not dishonor.

Jasmine and Angelica tended, comforted Tansy until the stomp of hooves thwarted their efforts, dividing them all.

Racks of drying herbs and roots were smashed. Their meal, a pottage of roots, was toppled. A spear was put to Usnea's back, spots of blood staining her gown, forcing her to move forward, to the center of the clearing.

Circling war-horses contained Jasmine and Angelica, with Tansy once again between them. War-horses mocked a dance, their huge hooves prancing, their heads lifting and straining, snorting of the fierce energy they wished to unleash.

Riders stabbed with their swords, aiming at the clustered women. Peasants, armed with pitchforks and sickles thrust at Usnea, forcing her through the circling parade to join the women huddled within. Dangerously, she passed through the procession of beasts, her skirt catching between soil and heavy hoof, ripping as she fell free.

Veri watched from above, breath held close, eyes wide. Not one of the women, who had been guide and friend, mother and sister, looked toward the tree where she hid. None gave the signal that she could come out of the lesson, that she could act and react. She had been taught too well. She did not to move, observed only.

It was a lesson.

Her heart beat rashly, her mouth sticky and dry. Fear.

It engulfed her, made her cold, on this ever so hot day, raised the hairs along her arms, at the tip of her spine. Goose bumps covered her, stretching across, from shoulder to shoulder, along her back. She shuddered as the priest cried out, "Where is she?" his voice sharp as the angles of his face. "Where is the child?" He railed.

Her! It had to be her, for she was the only child among the women.

All this, all this pain and suffering because he wanted her. She ached to jump, to stop all of this, holding back as she searched frantically, looking for some sign, some signal from her mentors.

With the aide of the others, Tansy rose to her feet, vainly trying to brush off the helping hands. Her hair of blazing fire long since gone gray, her eyes thickened, hidden behind a veil of jelled liquid, hindered her not. She was the Elder of the women; she would not be pushed aside. Despite the tremor of her arm, noticeable of late, now more so, she pointed an accusing finger at the men outside the circle of horses. She pointed as though the animated wall were nothing more than a cloud of smoke.

"How dare you come to this place, to disturb that which has made your families and your families' families well! We cannot do our work with fear rattling though our frames. Tell us that which you want and go on your way," she commanded, as though dressed in silks rather than grasses, and her empty hands held scepters. How tall the old woman appeared despite her diminutive size and hunched back.

"Witch!" The priest spat. He turned quickly from her, as he told the horsemen, "Take her; she shall hang. The rest burn, burn them here as they shall burn in hell! Do you hear me?" He shouted the last before any hesitation could take place, but still it was too late. The horses shied, sidestepped away; the peasants, with their pitchforks and sickles, racks and scythes, shifted rather than move forward.

An awkward moment as each questioned the strength of the priest as opposed to the strength of the Women. Who had more power, which would truly affect their lives?

Unaware the child he sought sat hidden mere feet away, that she glared at him with rising fury, the priest's own eyes glittered with the madness of the fanatic. Those on warhorses lifted their swords as the ragtag army of peasants prepared to plunge in and grab the women.

Veri's rage billowed, a silent rolling cloud, black as midnight. As though mirroring her turmoil, the air turned an eerie yellow, quieted, muting the jangle of the horses. Eyes widened. The priest screamed, breaking Veri's suppressed rage. Her voice called to the heavens, to the skies, to any force she could hail that would save her family. And with her

scream a screeching wind rose from nowhere, blew
fierce and hard. Hailstones the size of acorns tinged
against armor, bounced off heads and shoulders. Men
scattered, their fingers busy making the sign of the
cross from shoulder to shoulder, head to chest.

The women stood tall, as though no hail could
hurt them. Veri knew they were deep within
themselves, learning the feel of hail.

A lesson.

The men fled, chased by a raging priest. All
failed to see that Rose and Edith stood mere feet away,
watching all that took place. The two women emerged
from the mouth of the cave, bundling the other women
together, urging them toward shelter.

"Hurry!" Rose prompted Angelica, a girl only
just become a woman with menses, stood rooted with
fear, "Hurry!" Rose spoke as a mother, firmly, gently.

No light showed in the younger woman's eyes,
no recognition. Angelica had pulled too deep within to
be reached.

Usnea looked toward the tree, signaled to Veri
with a sharp nod of her head, signaling lesson over.
Time now to dissect and organize what was learned.

A spit of time was all it took to move from the
main cavern to a huge space further inside the caves.
Efficient and directed, they'd done what needed doing,
until they were settled deep in the heart of the earth,
far deeper than they had ever camped before.

A stream flowed through the space, bubbling
against the narrowing of rocks, bulging into a small
pool. There the water sat, a false calm before
narrowing, aggressive once more, a surging cascade,
wild and reckless, falling, falling to land with a
thunderous roar far below.

Beside the calm pool, the women circled a large
fire, their most precious possessions; bags of herbs,
pots and vials, lotions, potions, piled along one wall.
Each woman had a bedroll between herself and the
cold stone floor.

With no sense of daylight or evening star, they sat in council. The cadence of voices rose, fell, some bullying, others frail. None would sleep until conclusions were reached. None would answer to fatigue. 'Twas the way of the healers.

"Father Ignacious will claim the hail was the devil's aide," Juniper fretted. No one disagreed. All knew the bleakness of Father Ignacious's religion.

"Father Kenneth would argue that the Lord had come to our defense," Rose countered.

Again, no one disagreed. Each held respect for Father Kenneth, the portly friar who traveled in the name of his church, stopping with the women whenever he was near. Many an evening had been spent listening to his tales. Many an hour had been filled inspecting herbs and roots he'd found in other places.

Aye, they held the man in high regard, but not so much by any as by Rose. Though she tried hard to hide it, Rose leaned heavily toward the friar's teachings of the church and his God.

The same church as Father Ignacious's but a very different God.

The women themselves were not a spiritual group. They shied away from superstition or explanations beyond the practical. Though much was beyond explanation, they did not doubt there was a logical reason for everything. They sought understanding in cause and effect rather than some invisible master hand working its revenge and grace. This, more than anything, made them suspect to the outside world.

Unfortunately, things such as the hail, that very afternoon, were exceptionally hard to explain. It had fallen when the fields were ripe with grain, when there had been the promise of a full harvest. 'Twas the first such hopeful harvest in years. All had been in readiness for the gathering of the grain.

Each of the Women knew that some act of nature had created that hail as surely as they knew the peasants would need a more easily found reason for such a devastating blow to their lives.

Cause and effect. What was the cause of the act of nature? Though trusting it was there, the sisters could not define it. The peasants could. Whether God's protection or devil's aid, it was the attack on the Women in the Woods, The Healers, that had created a situation tantamount to famine.

Now what was to be done?

Angelica sat quietly, still deep within, despite the ministrations of the women. Tansy appeared feeble, her stand against the attack draining away whatever strength she'd stored. The rest made the decision. They must move on. It was too dangerous to stay amid such hatred and distrust.

"I'll not leave my home and those who still trust me to ease their pain and suffering." Tansy proclaimed, garnering just enough boost to utter her words before slumping back into a motionless heap.

Rose looked toward the elder. "If we go to the convent of Our Lady, 'tis only a day's journey for those in need. The sisters have a fine garden of herbs and healing plants."

Tansy shook her head stubbornly, "'Tis more than a day's journey come winter, even worse for those truly ailing. I am no Christian who heeds two gods under one name." She continued mumbling, interjecting the names of the only two priests the women knew.

A dejected silence plagued the others until Usnea, with a heartfelt sigh, lifted her bulky frame from the ground.

"Well, I am going to the east and then south. 'Tis told that the winter is not so harsh. My old bones would welcome a mild air."

"I will travel with you," Edith surprised the council by saying.

Although she was a well-respected member of the band, Edith was an unknown quantity to them. Not only had she joined them in an unusual way, but she had known a man as well, and known him in the most intimate sense.

The others had been brought into the group when babes or small children, spending their entire lives focused on healing. 'Twas no mistake that they were all women. Men were thought to be the antithesis of a healer, a distraction, not to be allowed within a healer's life lest they dissuade the women from their purpose. 'Twas another element that drew suspicion from the world. They were a society of women in a world that believed females needed the controlling hand of men just as people needed the guidance of the church.

Edith had neither trained since youth nor been celibate. She'd had a husband, birthed six sons, then lost them all, five years back, to a plague. As midwife in her village, she was the closest thing to a healer. She'd fought, strove, to save lives, losing one after another of her family and friends. The sense of futility nearly killed her where the plague had not. The Women had found her wandering aimlessly through the woods, searching and seeking these mysterious women of legendary lore.

"'Tis time we spread our skills about." She told the others, "Though known far and wide, 'tis not always easy to go a distance when your health is not with you."

"And what of those who do travel the miles?" Tansy taunted, "What of them when they arrive only to find no one here?" She tapped her rooting stick upon the ground, emphasizing her point in a way her weary voice could not. "I will not desert those in need."

Rose stood, moved closer to the fire, crouched down as if the flames would help her find the words she needed, though simple they turned out to be.

"I will go to the convent," She finally said, surprising no one, "to help those of a Christian persuasion who fear those with no faith."

"Christians?" Jasmine fairly shrieked, "Best not tell them you were with us! I would not care to see how you fare! I will go to the Scots. They look up to ones such as us. And I will take Angelica, for there she will be safe."

"'Tis cold and brutal in the land of the Scots," Usnea warned.

"I care not," Angelica announced, startling the group.

All looked toward Tansy.

"Tansy, you and Veri can come with me. Word will spread." Rose promised.

Once more, Tansy negated the suggestion with a shake of her head, though she said nothing.

"I will stay with her." Veri, small and delicate, despite her stubborn chin, spoke for the first time. She was the youngest, with the women since a babe. Born no more than eight harvests ago, she'd learned much. There was much for her to learn yet. Tansy's skills would be needed.

"They will come back and kill you both," Jasmine warned.

But it mattered not. All had been decided. Usnea and Edith to the southeast, beyond the town of London. Jasmine and Angelica would journey north to the Scots. Rose would go on her own to live in seclusion at the convent of Our Lady, while the oldest and youngest faced the trials of staying within the caves, within the woods.

CHAPTER 2 ~
IN THE YEAR OF OUR LORD 1216

Icy March winds batted against the stone of the castle. Damp seeped into every corner of every room and into every bone of Roland's inert body. It was a test, frigid and bitter, but one which he refused to fail.

So he lay, face down, arms flung out from his sides. A Christ-like impression as still as any statue laid out upon the numbing flagstone floor. Contours of the stone were imprinted upon his cheek. His muscles cramped painfully, knotted by the cold which had long ago worked its way into the depths of him. He had to piss like hell, the most earthly test of all, but he'd not move. He would stay as he was, prove to God and to all who dared to cross him that he was worthy to be called knight.

There had been moments, during the endless night, when he had questioned his right to the title of "Sir" Roland. Other times found him wanting one good reason to torture himself in this manner. Satan battling his defenses. In the end, he realized it was the only way to get where he wanted to go. It was the last ordeal, the last hurdle to the honor he had worked for since the meager age of seven, and dreamt of for many a year before then.

He would be Sir Roland, knighted as his father had been and his father's father before him. Valor would be his motto, chivalry his creed. Enduring this night of hunger, thirst a mere fraction of what he would face in the name God and all that was holy.

Therefore, Roland lay before God's cross, within the chapel of Dunstan Hall, home of his liege

lord, Lord Asquith. Home of his father's closest
friend. His debt of fasting had been paid, his body
stiffened into a permanent reminder of the cross he
would represent as a Knight Templar. Roland held to
his penance warmed by his heart and soul. Ready.

He heard it first, the creak of hinges that needed
oil, the sound of footsteps slapping upon the stone
floor as a man approached. This was not the first
visitor to come. The house was too full to allow such
peace, the night too long for others to fight the desire
to challenge his stillness. They came to inspect,
observe, whispering among themselves. Then there
were those, having started the celebrations early, who
were full of mischief and revelry. They arrived in
groups to taunt and test Roland's dedication to the
night.

In groups or in pairs, they never came alone.
This one did.

A man alone. He knew by the slap of each
sandaled step. He could hear the swish of fabric, rough
fabric, not the sliding glide of a silk gown, nor the
telltale slap of sword sheath against thigh. No, it was
neither man of battle nor gentle woman, but a priest.
Time for Roland's vigil to end.

Still, he did not move, would wait.

The black hem of a friar's mantle first came to
view, followed by the peek of portly sandaled feet.

"Roland?"

He dared not lift his head lest it seem that he
was easily pulled from his prayers. This could prove a
trick, a test, to see if he were sainted enough to follow
the calling.

"Roland, rouse yourself, 'tis I, Father Kenneth.
Time for you to ease your posturing and rise, bless this
day and bathe yourself of all impurities."

"Father Kenneth?" Roland asked, surprised that
this particular friar should be there; the one who had
stopped within his own home many a time, becoming
both teacher and guide to Roland when he was no more

than a child. It was auspicious indeed that Father Kenneth be here, this day, of all days.

"My father has sent you to see me into knighthood?"

"Yes, lad," Kenneth answered cautiously, "your father has sent me. But enough of this, there will be time enough for talk of your family. First, though, you must prepare yourself for this special day." The friar paused before adding quietly, "Then we will talk."

"Aye," Roland nodded, "matters of personal import must wait. Forgive me,Lord," Roland began his prayers, as Father Kenneth helped him gain his feet. It was no easy task, as his body had grown stiff and unbending from staying within one position for so many hours.

"The bath is a warm one, it will help ease the ache." Kenneth promised, enthusiastically adding, "it would not have been my choice, to face such an ordeal in such a season as this. If it were my place, I'd wait for late spring, or," he chuckled, "wait until mid-summer's day. Aye, that I would."

"No doubt," Roland admonished with his youthful zeal, "as it would take you a twelve month to finally make it through the night of penance, for you'd not find it in your spirit to keep your mouth silent for such a length of time!" Thus spoken, Roland rested an arm on the old man's shoulder. He'd have given it a squeeze, if his hand would have moved in such a manner.

The older man guided him through the chapel, out the side door, to a place in the hall.

"Piss here, lad," Kenneth instructed, pointing to a bucket within an alcove just beyond the chapel doorway, "shed all that is unholy within you."

"Aye, yes," Roland responded, with more eagerness than he thought fitting. The cold had numbed his brain as well, chilled his manly sense of the spiritual.

"It is the cold that makes the need so great."

"Aye," Roland sighed.

A page stood to the side, a young lad, who would become squire to Roland's knight. The page stood, as Roland had once stood, ready to do any bidding required of him. He would remove Roland's bucket, empty it, clean it, and return to help Roland don his attire of white. He would serve his newfound lord, fetching and bringing, taking on all tasks, no matter how small and insignificant. It was the way of learning. It was the way of yearning to be the one on the commanding end.

"How does my father go?" Roland finally asked, as he moved along the hall with Kenneth, "Has he come with you? Will he be here for this day?"

"Nay,"

Roland stopped, moving no further, stunned by the friar's reply.

As though to ensure Roland that he had not heard wrong, the portly friar shook his head as he crossed to the entrance of the bathing room.

"Nay?" Roland barked.

"'Tis what I said." Kenneth replied, "Now come, your bath awaits you." He urged Roland to the entrance of the bathing room.

Roland hesitated. It was his father's place to be there, to issue the blow, with the broadside of his sword, that would mark Roland a knight. It was a passing point in Roland's life, a coming of age, and the mark of his manhood. All his living family should be present, there to witness the ceremony, and there to join in the festivities that would last for days.

His father had paid a high price for the lavish display of food and entertainment. He had sent word that he was eagerly awaiting this day. What could have detained him? Was it that his son, his youngest, was only worth the coins it took to create such an event? Was not Roland, third son though he be, worthy of his father's presence?

"Stop, boy, do not think what your eyes are telling me you think. It was not in your father's heart to be away. He would give his life to be here, but it is not to be so. That is why he sent me, to see you through this day and to tell him, in marked detail, how it goes for you. He will be mightily broken to see how his absence has affected you."

"It does not affect me," Roland lied coldly.

"Aye, it does, but all will be made clear soon enough, for now come into this room. It is time we clean all evil and worldly thoughts from you."

Back stiff with cold and resolution, Roland crossed the threshold of the bathing room. Immediately, the warmth enveloped him, evaporating all thoughts from his mind. Sweet flames of a fire filled the huge hearth, coupled with the added warmth of braziers that bordered a copper tub filled to brimming with steaming heat. It beckoned him.

"If you're to bathe away your sins, as well as your stench," Father Kenneth wryly added, "It might as well be in warmth."

"That it might be," Roland agreed heartily, "and I should be grateful that a man so pleased by earthly comforts should be here to see me through this day."

"That you should. But before you look down from your grand height, remember the days I live between one place and another. Traveling may offer adventures, even for a simple friar such as myself, but it also offers many a cold night with little to no food. Tease as you will, but keep such thoughts in that thick head of yours."

"Kenneth?" Roland ventured, as he quickly stepped out of his clothes and into the heat of the water. "What is it you are not telling me?"

Kenneth considered his answer as he ensured the drying towels were warm; there was time enough to allow the lad a chance to wear his knight's spurs without sorrow.

Tomorrow.

Tomorrow Kenneth would tell Roland the whole of it. But for now, let the boy enjoy his moment of glory, his coming of age within the realm of chivalry.

"Well, man?" Roland demanded, "What is it that has you so forlorn and silent? What keeps you from speaking up?"

"Nothing," Kenneth lied, "but thoughts of the Women, the ones who were known to live in the woods."

"Them?" Roland perked up, for all wondered of the mysterious women of the woods. Tales of them flowed aplenty. Many a child had been known to behave for hours on the promise of such stories. Excitement such as this did not entirely die with childhood.

"Aye," Kenneth sighed, truly saddened with the thought. "Ignacious has sent them asunder with naught left but an old woman."

Forgetting his bath, Roland turned more fully around. "But I thought they had all vanished more than two years ago. You say there is still one left?"

"Aye, the eldest and an apprentice who is there to care for her. The old one will need it. She did not fare well this past winter."

"A child? She's more likely to be eaten than to survive enough to be of help!"

Kenneth tsked angrily, "Even a healer needs help with gathering wood for a fire, or moving about. You're nothing but a young pup, yet you could not rise from a cold floor without aide. Don't be so certain to fire darts toward those you know nothing about.

"As is, I think we should stop and gather them together when we go to meet your father."

Silence arced between friar and man, as Kenneth realized he had said too much, and Roland knew he was getting answers to his questions.

"My father is not well."

"We will speak of it tomorrow."

"No!" Roland barked, with command far beyond his age, "We will speak of it now! For if my father is near to dying, I will dedicate this day to him!"

"Then let us pray, and give this day unto your father."

Roland listened to the words, absorbed what his chilled brain had been too slow to gather before. His father did not come for he could not come. But he had not died. Not yet. For if he had, Kenneth would not be talking of the healer. Instead he spoke of the hag. That meant there was hope.

Tomorrow, they would set off for the home of the Women of the Woods. There would be no fortnight's worth of celebration. Not for Roland. It was time to seek his place in the world. To bid his father farewell. To welcome his brother into his rightful inheritance. For that would be the reason behind his brother's absence on this day. Edward would be there to take the lead of the family, if his father should die.

However, his father would not die. Not yet. Not before Roland returned, knighted.

When all was settled, then Roland would head for the Holy lands. In the name of all that is good, he would help to conquer, to win back from the heathens, what they never should have had.

CHAPTER 3 ~ THE ENEMY

Roland rounded a bend as Kenneth turned upon the seat of his mule.

"They will not be much farther." The friar called over his shoulder.

Roland grunted in response, plagued by loss, his thoughts a roiling mess of fury and despair. Near to home but not close enough. His father so close to death, he might not survive long enough for Roland's return.

His brother would not be there to greet him.

Edward, sensitive and caring, had turned to the cloth then relinquished it, as heir to their father's earldom. Murdered somewhere, here, on this hillside, in the shadow of St. Michael's Mount.

Murdered in the same manner their older brother had been murdered.

Less than a year ago, they had been a family, challenged each other to sword fights and chess while their father watched for fair play. All of it gone now. People taken too swiftly. Dreams destroyed on a quiet piece of land, near Oakland, the home of his youth.

Near the caves of the healers.

Roland spent his youth romping through these woods, scaling hillsides such a short distance away. If this had been the home of The Women of the Woods, Roland would have come up against them any number of times. As a lad, he certainly had tried. A boy's greatest fantasy was to track down those infamous women of spiritual darkness, to see them face to face and not bolt in terror. Roland had been no different than any other boy, when he was a boy.

A time long passed.

Kenneth, at the lead, broke into an opening in the wood, the sunlight like a beacon after the shadows of the leafy canopy. Roland followed, scanning the scene as he'd been scanning the trail during the whole of the journey.

Knights trained to keen awareness, to never be taken by surprise. How had his brothers, one the best of knights, the other an intense observer, been caught so unguarded within a pleasant meadow with its delightful bubbling stream?

The hillside backed off enough to create a quiet, sheltered place bordered by trees. Just such a place was responsible for his family's sorrow.

Just such a place?

Hairs rose along the nape of his neck, as the significance of the meadow tainted the day. His gaze shot from side-to-side, the surrounding curtain of trees from tips to base, the shallow stream that gurgled and ran through the center of the clearing. The course of water started farther up the rocky face of the mountain. It poured out from between two ledges to drop some twenty feet into a pool before flowing along into this quiet glen.

"This is where Edward was ambushed?"

Quietly, Kenneth looked about him, as though gaging the space for a morbid history. He finally answered with a mere, "Aye," nodding his head, as his normally recalcitrant mule, Homer, moved toward the stream.

"Is this not the same place where Hugh the younger lost his life?"

"Aye, that it is," Kenneth replied.

The friar's usual calm abraded Roland's restlessness.

"I wish to stop."

"Then do so. But I will not." Kenneth added calmly.

"You will do as I do!" Roland barked.

At this Kenneth did stop, turning in his saddle to look back at a fiercely scowling Roland.

"Are you commanding me?" Kenneth asked with humor.

Taking advantage of Kenneth's halting, Roland dismounted. "Aye, I am, for these woods are obviously not safe and I am your sole protector on this journey."

Kenneth's bark of laughter caused Homer to twitch his ears. Roland's scowl grew darker.

"Do you not trust that I have earned my gilded spurs, had the right to be called knight?" Roland quizzed.

"Nay," Kenneth denied, swallowing back any more laughter, "Nay, but do you not think that I have traveled farther with less arms and no harm? Do you think you are truly my soul protector? And in doing so, do you not think that you fail to trust in He who is the great protector of us all?"

"Did he protect my brother and my brother before him?"

With a deep sigh, Kenneth swung down from his beast. "Aye, he protected them in many battles, in many ways, but when it is time for a man to die, it is time." Kenneth led his mule to drink from the gurgling spring.

Roland stayed where he was, no longer focused on the friar. Instead, he looked about the clearing. 'Twould seem a pleasant place, but it was not. 'Twas a place of bad omen. A place of ambush and murder.

To have two brothers set-upon in one spot was not a measure of coincidence. Not in the same manner, in the same field, when there were no other attacks sited upon this place.

'Twas not coincidence.

A vile place, no more than an innocuous meadow. Short, coarse grass and newly-sprung wildflowers bordered by a stand of trees. No snapped branches, broken flower stems, or flattened grass.

Roland saw no sign of anyone preceding him, yet hairs rose on the nape of his neck.

He studied the shallow stream that fell between two ledges, from an opening high up a rocky slope. Water cascaded some twenty feet into a roiling pool. By the time it reached where he sat upon his horse, it was a lazy peaceful stream.

Peace was an illusion easily shattered.

This was the place of the healers, the witches. The ones the peasants both sought after and cowered from.

Those women had been ousted years ago, by the fanatic Father Ignacious and his sense of righteousness. It had been a brutal scattering, a legendary moment that provided two ghosts as memorial; a grisly old woman and a child.

Neither was accountable for the shudder of apprehension that rippled along Roland's spine. Nor where those the ghosts he wished to see.

It was his brothers he wanted. Edward. Howard. Their deaths, as brutal as the old women's and still fresh, hurt.

Roland over rode the pain, raw and open, with fury. He let it flow through his veins, a white hot fire of anger. If any specter were to appear, he wanted it to be his two older brothers, attacked and butchered in this quiet little place, to tell him who felled them. Retribution was his due.

A time for vengeance.

Despite its deceptive innocence, Roland knew the meadow held the key. But where? How had his brothers been taken by surprise? How could he, a green knight, having earned his spurs no more than a fortnight before, find the answers?

Spring rains had washed away the blood. No evidence remained. Still, Roland studied the land, the shade of the trees, the mountain side. Something wasn't as it should be; he knew it, waited for unconscious clues to surface.

On the ledge, where the stream sprang from the hillside, he noted crooks and crevices, dark shadows. He watched the edge of the forest, the sway of each branch. Nothing unusual. As he pivoted, to look behind him, body twisted toward his left, his head snapped back.

The ledge.

Of course.

It was the ledge.

There, a shadow stood, alone, nothing to cause it, no rocky overhang or bush. Just a dark shade.

He cursed. Knew he had revealed himself with treacherous intent. He feigned disinterest. As though to look farther down the path, he settled in his saddle, looked straight ahead, all the while his gaze angled to that darkness. In a furtive movement, quick as a blink, what had been a dark outline became a figure. It bent low and darted through a fissure in the rock.

Got you!

Roland bit back a yelp of victory. It was too early for that. The confrontation was yet to come. And it would. He relished the moment, was prepared for it.

He was glad to see Kenneth already mounted and ready to ride. Not wanting to bring attention, should anyone be watching, he kept his voice low as he instructed, "Friar, go ahead of me with a steady gate. As soon as you are out of sight, ride as hard as that mule will take you and go get help."

Alarmed, the man looked to him.

"Calm, father, calm. We are being watched."

Kenneth nodded a stiff jerk of his head and kicked his mule in the gut. No movement. "Now is no time to be stubborn." He kicked again.

Roland leaned, brushed the dirt, revealing a stone. Kenneth looked at him and cringed, as he repeatedly dug his heels into the animal.

With a flick of his wrist, Roland sent the stone whizzing through the air to hit the mule with a sharp thwack. The animal took off, Kenneth clinging to its mane.

Roland laughed, a good bit of fun between friar and knight, all the while excitement blasted through him in a heady swirl of emotion, pumped his blood, filled him with a reckless, billowing energy to be unleashed against his attackers. Sword in hand, he remounted Spirit, aware that the person on the ledge was a lookout, the watch, a signal to his enemies.

The last of the Montgomery brothers had arrived.

But this brother would not be taken. He had the advantage. He knew they were there, that they were coming.

He was prepared.

Roland pitched forward with such force he splayed across Spirit's right shoulder.

An arrow from behind. Close range. It was all he could think, analyze. His chain mail had been pierced, as had his leather jerkin. The attack was from close range.

He tried to turn, to see his enemies, but was knocked sideways, as another arrow lodged deep within his arm. He tightened his thighs, the only hold that kept him mounted.

He had faced the mountain, certain the attack would come from there. He had been wrong.

A mighty blow sent him straight over, off the wide seat of Spirit. His head crashed against the ground, the only part of his body to break the fall. His foot twisted in the stirrup. Dazed, he fought to get loose, as Spirit reared and danced against the attackers, forced them to keep their distance, dragging Roland in his wake.

Roland had come to seek answers, to ensure at least one Montgomery man survived. He needed time, but there was no more time.

He had not been prepared.

CHAPTER 4 ~ THWARTING EVIL

"I knew there would be trouble, I've felt it!" Veri scrambled through the cave toward a channel that would take her lower into the mountain to where Tansy mumbled, huddled by the fire.

Veri didn't listen to the old woman. There was no time. She had to think, hard, of what she could do to stop what was about to happen.

"'Tis long past time that you be 'feeling' things, young lady." Tansy's voice rose so there would be no missing her rantings, "And a fine thing, as 'tis your man out there. He'll be near to death he will, mark my words, he'll be near to death." Her cackle broke through Veri's frantic search. "But he'll not die. Not yet. Not until he's yours and you have a dozen little ones grown big and tall. He'll not die."

"Please," Veri pleaded, "not now. I need help. I've no way to stop them when they fall upon him." She nearly wept, "And they will, as they have in the past with those others. Please, Tansy," she crouched before the old lady, "help me, think, think of what I can do! This time, when I know what is about . . . "

"Wake your beast," Tansy told her, as though it was an obvious solution.

"Cin?" Veri's head shot up, her face turning toward the darkness of the tunnel.

"Why else do you keep him with his foul stench?"

Veri did not wait to listen to the old healer's words. The idea was planted and it was sound. She hurried to the tunnel, pulled herself through the narrow opening, crawled on her belly, for the space allowed no more. It was a downward journey, widening slightly then, suddenly, amid the flurry of bats' wings, the pungent odor of their droppings and the obnoxiously foul scent of bear, she knew she was in the cavern.

"Cin! Cin!" She called and hurried, blindly but knowingly, through the black space. Oomph, she fell over a huge mass of fur.

"They say people make rugs of beast like you." She pushed herself up to crawl across the animal. "But I would think they'd smell too wicked." She kept moving. "Come," she spoke, as though the animal would understand. "We have to help."

On a snuffled snort, the bear lumbered toward Veri, its huge claws scraping against the cavern floor. She could feel its fetid breath behind her, as she struggled through another small opening.

"We must help." Veri fretted, feared that the attack would happen before she could do anything.

She'd been helpless the last time, just weeks past, when two other men had been set upon. That time she had known of the rugged band of men who hid in the woods. She had also seen the riders approach. Her error had been in failing to connect the two until the attack that left her meadow littered with dead bodies.

This time, she would do what she must to stop it.

She broke into daylight, saw the lone horseman dangling by one ankle, foot caught in a stirrup. His mount turned and twisted upon powerful hind legs, pawed at the air, waged battle against three armed men, to protect the one even as he dragged him about.

She stood frozen, not knowing what to do, helpless, hopeless. She heard the thud when the young knight freed himself and rolled from the prance of his horse. He pulled his broad sword from its sheath, steadied the weight of it with the hand of an injured arm.

Veri watched, as she tried to take it all in. Two assailants backed away from the vicious hoofs of the horse. A third tried to approach from the left, but the young knight saw him, turned to counter the attack. A movement, near the trees, pulled Veri around. There was a fourth man, in the shadows, his bow raised, its arrow aimed straight at the horse that continued to pivot, front legs high, a dance both majestic and deadly.

"Nooooo!" Veri shrieked, as she saw the arrow fly, heard its whistle, the soft thud of purchase, the twang as it bit deep into the animal's flesh, near to his heart or in it, she could not tell. She heard it scream, saw it stagger. Bumps rose along her arms, up her neck, as the horse's squeal of pain echoed against the mountain. In tandem the earth jolted with the thump of the great powerful animal as it fell hard, on top of his owner.

The man's chest would be crushed, his legs shattered, a miracle if he survived.

Was the horse dead, too? She had to see, had to check. Her mind raced, her heart too stunned to feel.

Senseless deaths, again, over and over again, at the hands of these . . . these . . .

Veri's fear fled. She forgot danger, the men, her own animal at her side. Fury bristled her rigid and straight. Without warning, the wind swirled a wild riot of bent trees and whirling debris. The age, size, number of her enemies mattered not. Cin's ferocious snarl, fed her belligerence. Celtic blood throbbed with the call of battle as she lifted her chin high in challenge and let loose her own wild warrior's scream.

The men didn't move, not at first. She almost laughed at the sight of them. They stood helpless in disbelief and shock, hair standing on end.

She knew her power, knew of the terror she instilled. Let them believe her a ghost, an apparition from the underworld that had come to get them. Let them think she had summoned the wind that pelted them with twigs and leaves.

Their mothers should have warned them of such dangers when they were mere boys playing at their cruel games. The little people will get you, the witches will turn you to salt. Taunts of childhood. Let them think she was that mystical wrath. She released another scream to screech along their spines with cold, terror filled, chills.

As one, the ruffians ran, scrambled, leapt upon their horses, allowed the animals to drag them in their wake when they could not manage to get astride. Veri ran after them, cried warnings that they would be swallowed up in what they had done to the world. The creature would do to them what they did to others and worse.

The fight hit fast, burned out as quickly. Veri could not keep up, left Cin to continue the chase as she stopped, stood, panting, crying, wiping tears from her cheeks with angry swipes.

Images flashed in her mind, inspired by this second heartless attack. It was a brutal reminder of the priest's assault against her people. The rampage of men on horses, the clink of armor, the billow of Iganicious's cape when they had attacked the healers. Veri closed her eyes against the memory, but the pictures continued to play.

Tansy, shoved to the ground by the point of a spear. Rose's hand crushed under the hoof of a blood crazed stallion. Violet and Chamy shocked into the depths of themselves, never to recover.

Veri had witnessed it all, hidden in the canopy of a tree. She had been a child then. Too young to fight, to help. Not that the elders had been any more successful.

Helpless fury, dormant from that time to this, shot from her in a scream, released a rage held tight. Her throat opened, her open face raised to the sky, as sound poured from her, high and piercing, until nothing was left within. Her legs buckled. She sank to the ground, bowed her head and sobbed.

A snort, an explosive sound of pain, snapped her head around to the carnage left behind.

It wasn't possible.

Another snuffle.

She shook her head and saw the twitch of an ear.

Could it be?

She rose up on her knees, afraid to believe. Yet she knew, suddenly realized that this time, this one time, she had not been too late. The horse, at least, was alive. Thanks be to that which both gave life and took it.

Veri edged over to the animal, quiet in her way. She didn't want to spook it. It was a dangerous moment, for he struggled to roll away from the man pinned beneath him.

"Whoa, boy," Veri crooned, "Quiet yourself, let me look at you."

Wild- eyed, the animal stilled, its sights set on Veri and her approach. It shook its head, lifted its muzzle, as though to warn that she should use caution in coming closer, but it no longer fought to rise, stayed curled upon its legs like a huge dog.

The man's legs were still beneath the animal but Veri thought it little to worry about now. The worst of the damage had been done. If the man was even alive, it would be worse to have the horse move too quickly, twist what was already, surely, broken.

Crooning, murmuring, in a language only the healers knew, Veri's voice floated through the air like a calming herb upon the beast. She reached it, reached out a hand, to touch where the arrow still pierced the chest.

It had missed the heart. Still, she was not anxious to pull the weapon from his flesh, lest the blood spurt forth and drain the animal too quickly of its life. For now she needed the stoppage. She stroked its neck, whispered into its ear, as she guided it to stand, slowly, carefully. The animal seemed to understand her concern, for he watched her carefully, followed her directions.

She told him of his injury; of how good it was the arrow missed the heart. She explained why she left the arrow in its place. She apologized for not being better prepared. She should have reached them sooner. She explained about the drop in the land, just beyond the trees, so easily missed because of the undergrowth, and how men could hide there without anyone the wiser.

She had known of it, she told the animal, as she led it just far enough away from its master that she could get to the fallen man. She had known, but didn't know what to do. She had no idea when anything would happen. Who could imagine that they would do something like this again? Could the beast? Surely not, for it was not, truly, in the nature of man, to do such things to each other.

Was it?

Spirit nodded and flipped his head, as though he listened to all her words and tried, in his own way, to convey his astonishment and dismay, and all the while they were both aware of the still figure beside them.

Veri looked at the man, then back to Spirit.

"I'd best see to him."

Spirit raised his head then lowered it, then let it drop even further, as he touched his nose to the foot of the man, nudged it as if to awaken the fallen fellow.

"Nay!" Veri's voice rose for the first time since she'd approached the horse, "Nay, you must be gentle with him. After taking such care to get your hulking mass off him, it would do no good to hurt him with a shove."

As she spoke, she bent down onto her knees, and leaned over the knight. She had never tended a male before, but it took her less than a moment to realize one injured body was not so different from another.

With deft, assured movements she ran her hands knowingly over his body, his chest to see if it were caved in enough to impale a lung. She felt a faint lift of his ribs, of breath taken in. She could feel a gentle brush of air from his mouth when she put her cheek to his lips.

Huge lumps formed in three places on his head, a horrible bruise above his left eye. He had two arrows planted in his body. One imbedded in his arm, at the shoulder, the other through his back, out the front. Both worried her, for she knew he had to be moved, and quickly, but she did not know how those arrows were situated in his body. The depth of a blade of grass could make the difference between survival or not.

The horse had already moved away, as if it knew Veri needed space to move around his master. A horse with such senses still intact, despite an arrow within its breast, was well enough to help relocate the injured. She would break off the length of the wooden shafts, but decided against pulling the arrows out too quickly. Again, it would be best to wait until she had bandages handy, herbs to clot the blood, and a sharp blade should the arrow need to be cut from the wound.

Assured of her decision, Veri turned back to the man, and looked where she had not wanted to look before. His legs. She kneeled beside his thigh and stared in astonishment. There was a dip in the land. He had the good fortune to land snuggly within it.

She checked the length of his limbs, and laughed with surprise when she realized his legs had not been badly hurt at all. One ankle was twisted, broken surely, but that was the extent of it.

Nothing, so far, seemed beyond her measure. Except Tansy. Veri had the old Healer, Tansy, to look after, as well as this man and she couldn't get him into the upper caves. That would be impossible. So she would have two to care for at opposite ends of a honeycombed network of caverns.

She closed her eyes against what she knew had to be done. She had held off doing so for far too long.

It was time to summon Rose from Our Lady's Convent. Rose would come and get Tansy, and take her back to the convent.

Tansy would fight it, had done so since Father Ignacious's attack, when all the other healers had headed for the safety of the church. But Tansy had come to be too much for Veri to handle. She was getting old, peculiar, living in a world of dreams and illusion that Veri did not understand.

Rose would know what to do.

Your man . . .Veri looked down at the knight beside her, as Tansy's words whistled through her mind.

Her man indeed.

Such words were proof of the elders drift from sense. Of all people, Tansy knew healers did not marry. It was forbidden. Men distracted women from their duties.

Besides . . . Veri looked at the figure, prostrate before her. He was, most definitely, a grown man. She was still young, not yet a woman. The world would have to flip-flop before they would be connected.

But she was connected. Fate had dictated she be his healer. In that Tansy had been correct.

Not until he's yours and you have a dozen little ones grown big and tall.

Feeble and confused. That's all there was too it. It was time to overcome Tansy's obstinance, and get her into the care of the convent.

Veri would think of Rose, imagine her on the road to the caves and Rose would come.

How?

Veri shook her head. She didn't have the slightest idea how it worked. She didn't need to understand. She just had to do it.

She thought of Rose.

* * * * * * * * *

Dreams and reality twined, as Roland fought to open eyes weighted with a heavy languor. A part of him didn't want to fight the lassitude, but only a small part. Curiosity won in the end.

Slowly, he lifted sleep-weighted lids to the awareness of firelight and a thick, low hanging haze of smoke. A figure crouched before the fire, swayed upon the balls of the feet, while tending to something. It was not an awkward squat, but a smooth melody of motion, a dance that caused an eerie hunched and menacing shadow upon a wall. Beyond that there was naught but deep, unfathomable darkness without break of starlight or campfires farther afield.

Alarmed he had woken so slowly, that he had no idea where he was or why he was there, Roland closed his eyes to fight his way to a memory, anything that could put him in this place. Every time he caught an edge of thought, reality dissolved into dream. He gave up, opened his eyes and focused, hard, to define his surroundings.

The ground beneath him was soft, a pallet of sorts, upon the earth. Acrid smoke the predominant scent, but there was another, far less palatable smell of rotted fish and damp fur. The identity of it was no more than a noxious flirt with awareness, but he knew the smell.

Eyes shut tight, he tried to catch the flickering images that skirted the edges of wakefulness. They refused, stayed just beyond his mind's eye. Thwarted, Roland looked about for more clues.

The grotesque, yet sensuous shadow moved upon an irregular continuous stone wall. The floor beyond his pallet smoothed dirt.

Jolted by sound, Roland realized his senses were coming back, one after another. First vision, then smell and now sound. They had all been there, in his dreams, so much there that he had not noticed them.

He did so now.

A powerful rumble of water, tumbling from a formidable drop to crash in the distance, constant and strong. It created a dampness, a mist of air. Through that, a voice moved from humming to soft indistinguishable words, as if both were an integrated part of a melody.

It was the voice of a woman, neither old nor young, but a female for a certainty. The music of voice and water gave new credence to the dance- like sway of the figure.

Confused, Roland turned his gaze back to the figure by the fire. Would she be hideously ugly when she turned to face him? He worried about that for a moment. Childhood fears and anticipation lingered with the dreamlike hangover.

Where was he? Why was he here? In a cave. He knew that now, with the shape of the stone walls, the damp, the smell of rotting fish, so much like bears.

Caves . . . caverns . . . bears . . . Pictures shot into his mind, images of a figure on the side of a cliff, an attack, his horse Spirit, reeling and falling and the glimpse of a bear, just as all went black.

There had been an attack, but unlike his brothers, he had not been left to rot within the meadow. Someone had brought him to the caves, to the witches.

He darted a look at the figure bent over the fire.

A witch or the servant child?

As if on command, she swiveled around, but he could see nothing for the light came from the fire behind her.

"You are awake." Her voice soft, melodious, swirled about him.

"You," he tried to say that she spoke English, for English was not the language she had been using, but he could not speak, was suddenly aware of the dryness of his throat, the burning of his body and the aches. He hurt all over. One more sense to come into focus, pain, and this one directly related with the female's awareness. She must be a witch to cause such agony with one look.

One glance and every manner of physical misery swept over him. He moaned, too pained to be embarrassed by the weakness.

The witch started to croon, like a mother to a child, soft, lyrical, in that other language, as if the sound would counter his moan. And it did, it soothed, dangerously so. To affect his suffering with mere utterings was the work of the devil. But he could not move, had neither strength nor desire to do so. Instead, he lay still, listened as he watched her approach, a backlit shadow of a figure. Small, so very small that she could almost be of the little people.

As she drew near, she carried the vessel she had stirred when he first saw her by the fire.

"I have been too long in preparing this," she soothed in English. "There were not enough roots. I had to find more. It took too long." She knelt before him, terrifying him, entrancing him, "You are in pain, the draught has worn away."

She tried to put the vessel to his lips, but he pushed it away. With a "tsk" she sat back on her heels, tilting her head to the side. "It would have been better if you'd not fully wakened. You are going to be difficult now."

In God's name he would be, but did not say so. Though desperate for a drink, he was just as desperate not to take anything this woman offered.

"Let me see you," It was difficult to speak with his mouth so dry, but he made himself understood, for she tilted her head even further as though she was thinking through his question. With sudden understanding, she shifted, pivoted on the balls of her feet, allowed the light to come at her by the side.

The child.

Roland released his breath. He was not afraid of the witches, certainly, but he was wary. The child was another matter. A victim, a mere pawn for their use. He would rescue her from these women, who tied children into their ways.

As thoughts of witches flooded his mind, images of thwarting them blossomed like a dream. He would whisk the child away. He would tuck her within his mantle, both of them riding away upon Spirit, as the old harpies wept and moaned, gnashed their teeth in frustration.

He would take the child to Oakland where none could harm them, for he was a great knight of a great family and honored house.

The girl had shifted back, readjusted the vessel in her hand, when something within the fire leapt and spit. A mere piece of coal but it caught Roland's imagination in much the way his knightly dreams had. The old women could be there, within the cavern, hidden in the darkness, forcing the child to tend to him and do their bidding. He peered into the shadows, looked, wondered. There, beyond the wall of darkness. They could be there.

"The others?" He questioned.

She put the ewer to his lips and he realized he could not, after all, fight her. It was foolish to try. If she had wanted to poison him, she would have done so already, for this was not the first time she had fed him the brew. He remembered it well from his dreams. So he drank the bitter liquid and prayed he'd come to no harm.

"What others?" she asked, as she administered to him, helped him to drink in small amounts.

"The witches?"

The container was pulled away as a frown formed between her brows.

"Do you know of witches?" She asked.

The bitterness of the potion puckered his mouth, increased his thirst. It was even more difficult to speak. With a start, the child mumbled something, then reached for a pot, pulled a rag from its mouth and put the spout to Roland's lips.

"It is water steeped with herbs. The plants help to ease your thirst."

As he drank, she grumbled about distractions and a wandering mind. As Roland listened, the world shifted and changed. The child seemed to expand, the darkness beyond held no significance except for the sound of water rushing and falling. He thought them to be within a pool, yet not wet. Peculiar, yet not so. He laughed at the complex game of his thoughts, and then, quite suddenly, he felt better. Magnificent. In fact, his pain receded almost as swiftly as it had come upon him. He felt his weight lift, his body float.

He smiled stupidly, wanting to tell the girl and ask if she floated, too, but all that came out was an inane laugh.

"Oh," she breathed, "You must not dream yet. You have not told me of the witches. I know nothing of them, have only heard stories. I had thought, mayhap, you have seen one?"

Roland looked to the girl, remembered what it was like to be a child, feeling halfway as though he were going back, traveling, to his boyhood. A time of dreams and sweet fears and dangling one's feet in streams.

He imagined her running through fields, picking wildflowers, shuddering over tales of ghoulish women. There was nothing to fear in this child. She was just that, a young girl, all alone, all alone, all . . .

"Sweet child," he murmured with a smile, as he drifted back into those dreams that were not sleep, yet not wakefulness either.

At times he could hear her move about, hum, speak to herself and then those sounds would twine with his dreams, illusions of swaying, grotesque monsters upon the walls. He must save her from evil, but his body, so light before, was now weighted down.

He could not move, had not the will to fight the lethargy.

He dreamt a bear nuzzled him, as though to roll him over. That nearly roused him, for he thought of the child. He must protect her from fiends and bears and hags. He must protect her.

Instead, he sank deeper into sleep.

CHAPTER 5 ~ COAL MAKER'S HUT

"You will come with me!"

The sleeping beast had woken and now she must deal with it. The fault was hers.

With a heartfelt sigh, Veri glanced over her shoulder at the huge mass of a man, slumped against the paltry doorway of their shelter, skin as clammy and white as the belly of a fish. She was amazed that the simple hut didn't give under his weight.

Their shelter, an empty charcoal maker's hut, was no more than a bundle of reeds roped together at the top, splayed at the bottom, with a modest framed door. Far too small for the man to stand within, barely room for his pallet and the small rock- rimmed fire. As it was, he had to lie in a curl along the wall of the hut, to fit without his legs dangling over the threshold.

A gentle rain fell behind him. He'd only been off his pallet for the breadth of time it took her to toss out his old bedding and arrange the fresh, which was no time at all. She'd had the new bedding ready before he had woken. Still, here he was, drooping like a water- starved leaf, demanding they pick-up and travel for days.

Obviously, size and age were no measure of the ability to reason.

Patiently, Veri corrected him, as she wished his people would return to take him. "You are going nowhere."

Weak though he was, he managed to show affront. "You are a slip of a girl to be telling me what to do."

"Aye," she agreed, for it was so, "a slip of a girl who has not been shot with arrows nor hit with great chunks of rock that knocked sense straight out of me."

His scowl reappeared.

Leaning over from where she knelt before the fire, Veri grabbed a cloth, dipped it in a basin of water and wrung it out, giving herself time to think. She was so small and he so big, how was she to get him to do what she commanded?

"I have to return to Oakland." The whole structure shuddered when he slumped down further, speaking to himself more than her. "Yesterday was too late."

"Oakland." Veri breathed. He'd talked of Oakland incessantly. Whispered of it, shouted of it, in his dreams and again upon waking. Before he had the strength to move at all, he had told her of his home, the places he'd been, the ways of others.

He didn't know, nor could she tell him, that his people were coming for him. Rose and Kenneth promised a message would be sent to Oakland. Some wayfarer spotted a wounded knight in a coal maker's hut.

A child sharing that hut, such as he knew her to be, could not possibly know this.

Frustrated, she knelt beside him, mopped the sweat from his forehead. "No importance can be met by a dead man or by one who will never find health again. You should still be abed, allow your wounds and your head time to mend."

"There is no time for that!" Impatiently, he grabbed her wrist, "I must be home. You will come with me, to see that I don't die."

Aye, though he didn't know it, Rose and Kenneth planned for this, so she could tend to him and to his father.

"If you wait even so much as another day, you will fare better." And your people will be here. She hoped.

"I have not another day. I must leave now and no later."

"Then you must leave alone and die."

Silence sat between them, as Veri's words hung within the air, a tangible thing. Roland laid his head back against the archway, Veri kept hers bowed.

Uncertainty plagued her. She could not chance his seeing it in her eyes. If he tried to leave, she would follow. There would be no choice.

She looked at him, closely, and knew.

It was in his eyes. He was foolish enough and then some. The elders had warned her of such things when treating men. They knew little of caring for themselves, and fought the care of others.

So he would die. He would be overcome with fever and he would die when he was so close to reaching his goal.

The picture was quite clear within her mind. He would stagger and fall, his body dripping with his own sweat, carrying with it every measure of strength he had. Animals would smell the coming of death and track him. He'd not be able to fight them off.

Bears claws! She would have to follow him, leaving no one here to be found.

Or, she would have to stop him.

Anger at his inane behavior had her by its teeth, a stubborn, flailing fury of frustration. She had to move, for she was too angry to sit near and not speak her thoughts. She would take action to stop him, knowing he would make her pay for thwarting him.

So be it. Once she calmed, she would set him to rights.

Roland took her arm, halting her. With a keen look, eyes too knowing for one so ill, he assessed her as he asked, "You were the one, the only one, to tend to me when I was ailing."

Veri stilled, trapped by his question, wishing someone would come and take him to this place, Oakland. Someone who cared for him, would care for him. So she could go back, safely, to the caves and her own life.

It was most important he not think her one with the healers. It was imperative she deny being who she was, an impossible task, one that barbed her temper.

"There was not overly much to it," she averred, pulling against his hold. "Not much other than bathing the wounds and watching."

"But you were alone?"

"Aye," she twisted her arm, trying to wrest free, truly afraid. "I was on my own."

"And you know of these things," he gestured around the shelter, "herbs and roots and healing foods?"

Defensively, Veri did pull free. He had not liked her healing foods. Had asked for meat which Veri refused. Healers did not eat meat.

"All females know of such things. It is what we are taught." She snapped, stepping across him to walk outside where there was air to breathe, and lightness of day. Roland followed, intent on his purpose.

The rain had turned to a drizzle, coating them each in glistening dew.

"There is truth to that, but you are no more than a child, with more talent than most women. I have need of that talent, Veri. If it is not too late, then my father will have need of your skills." Roland stood behind her, a huge man next to her childishness, "walk with me, to Oakland, come with me to see if my father still fares with life."

Veri frowned again, frustrated by his rescuers' delay.

He wasn't playing fair, vexing her with worry for his parent, with no way of knowing her predicament.

Spinning around she snapped. "It is cobweb thoughts to think you will be of any use without rest."

Roland laughed, "Listen, child," he emphasized her youth, hovering over her with his hugeness,

unstable as it was, "Trust that I am the elder and
therefore know far more of these things than you!"

With a snort, she marched past him to duck into
the shelter.

"You will come with me!" Roland demanded,
following her into the cramped space.

Able to stand where he had to scrunch his tall
body, she tried to glare, but tears weakened the affect.

"Selfish brute." She stamped her foot, as close
to a tantrum as she had ever been. "You give no care
to the time and effort to bring you this far. Such a
short time since I found you, not even a full course of
the moon.

"If you wish to do yourself an injury, then do
so. But do not command me to leave my home, the
ways that I am about . . ."

"You will have a home with me, a family. Why
that isn't call enough for you is beyond my ken, but"
he replied, obviously stung that she would think him
selfish, "if you were to know the need of my journey,
you would be hastening us on."

"Would I?" She asked tartly, wondering if he
could see her hesitation.

He had been fine company, this past day of
wakefulness, when not going on about returning to his
beloved Oakland.

With a great huff, she sat on the far side of the
fire, toyed with a bowl, smoothed the dirt surrounding
the glowing coals. Thinking, thinking how best to
thwart him.

Suddenly, certain, she reached for her pots,
taking a pinch of herbs from one, a palm full from
another, tossing them into a small kettle filled with
simmering water. She decided to distract him.

"Tell me more of this place you call Oakland,"
she asked, as she mixed her brew disturbed by his
frown.

She knew that look well. Strangers were not
used to a child trained to listen, to assess and make

decisions. With all she accomplished caring for him, she expected better from her patient.

"Well!" she snapped causing Roland to laugh.

"Aye, I will tell you," he promised, as he settled down upon his newly made bed. Veri handed him a wooden bowl filled with her herb mixture. As he held it, she added a chunk of honey followed by ladle of hot water. Head tilted thoughtfully to the side, she watched him sip the brew.

"Ahh," he sighed, "Once again you feed me with comforting draughts," his voice was lazy and calm, "And, as you have cared for me, so I have vowed to take care of you."

Veri laughed. She could not help it, and felt sorry when she saw his hurt scowl. As a peace offering, she poured more of her mixture into his bowl, watching as he drank it down.

"I have no need of being cared for." She explained.

"No need?" Roland raised his eyebrows; "Everyone has that need, to be cared for, thought of, loved." The last uttered gently, the word itself a precious thing. "Besides, would you not prefer a home where the rain won't leak over your head? Where it is not possible for animals to prey upon you when you sleep? Where, should you fall ill, there would be another to tend to you?

"And the clothes! Delicate lace, smooth silks and plush velvet. Warm clothes, with a fine weave."

Insulted, Veri looked to her own perfectly serviceable dress. "There is naught wrong with my weaving. I am very good with wool!"

Roland chuckled softly, "Wait until you see the gowns that I will have prepared for you. Then, you will know what I speak of."

"I have no need of another gown. This one still fits well enough."

Roland relaxed fully, stretching out as best he could, looking at the ceiling of their humble abode, as though seeing the things he spoke of.

"I will take you with me, to the Holy Lands. You will come and I will be your guardian, a brother and you will be a younger sister."

"The Holy Lands?"

"Aye, just as I have vowed to take care of you, I have vowed to go on crusade. We will leave as soon as my father is well."

"You make many vows." Veri stated thoughtfully.

"Aye, and those I speak of are not the only vows I have made." He yawned roundly, stretching his large body as much as space permitted, before continuing. "When you found me, I was on my way to Oakland, where it is said my father lies near to death."

"Ah, yes," Veri's brow furrowed in thought, "You spoke of your father's failing."

"That I did, for, if he still lives," Roland's tongue tangled on words. Slurring slightly, he continued, "I would have you tend him."

Veri watched as the man's eyelids drifted closed. He fought against the drowsiness, opening his eyes wide with a snap, rolling to his side as though that would aide him in remaining alert. He reached for the bowl of herbs she had fed him, bringing it close, so he could smell the contents. Lifting his head, he stared at her as his arm dropped, spilling the last sips onto the dirt floor. With effort, he raised himself onto his elbow, his sleepy gaze focusing on Veri. 'Twas not so sleepy as to hide the anguish within.

"Sleeping potion," he growled. "You have done it!" The herbs made his tongue clumsy but did nothing to quiet his rage. "First, my brother's killers . . . attack . . . then you . . . a mere snip . . . You. Will. Pay. For this . . . I will . . ." With a thud, his body fell back upon the pallet.

"Just one more day, that was all I asked of you. One more day." She murmured, wondering if she should be gone before he returned to wakefulness. Perhaps, if his people didn't arrive by tomorrow, she could find his horse, have him waiting, a conveyance to carry him home.

Or, perhaps she could make him sleep until his health returned.

Then again, perhaps not. She doubted he'd take another sip from her.

It was a shame, for she could make him feel so very much better. If only Tansy were there. She'd know what to do, how to handle this man. But Tansy wasn't near. No one was near.

She grabbed the lambskin bag, tossed it over her shoulder, ducked out of the hut. Something grabbed her hair, hurled her out onto the wet grass.

The shock robbed reason, her breath whooshed from her lungs as a boot collided with her stomach. Her small hands proved meek protection against the onslaught.

"You," the assaults lessened but for one, "tried" another resounding hit, "to kill him!" Attack, rant, kick, brutal, unwarranted punishment.

Worse than any nightmare, the yip and snarl of dogs twined with the sound of horses dressed in fancy metal.

One tug and she dangled, by her hair, in a man's hold. He was big and fierce, with dark hair that covered from head to chin, his dark eyes and upturned nose the only signs of a face. With leather- gloved fist he back handed her, sent her flying back to the ground.

Blood dribbled down her face, along her neck, as she tried to rise to her hands and feet. She needed to cough, gingerly tried to, causing more blood to bubble up, conscious of the sound of those horses, those fancy dressed horses.

"It's his bag." Someone railed. Veri opened one eye, the other already swollen shut, to see a skinny

man with leather jerkin lean over to pick up the
gathering bag she had borrowed.

This was worse, so much worse, than the attack
on the women by the priest and his gang of peasants.
The steady rain left no room for hail, not that such a
minor thing would stop these men. The only one who
could stop them, who would, was peacefully sleeping
by her own hand, because she didn't want to argue
with him.

She was going to be killed, brutally.

Huddled on the ground, trembling, Veri curled
up, an arm around her middle, another over her head,
prepared for blows that never came. Tremors racked
her body, worse with the waiting, the fear, of the next
assault.

"What have you done with him?" A mountain of
a knight, with metal plated chest, loomed over her.
"Can you make him better?"

Without warning, the ground heaved. Trees
groaned with the twisting, boulders rolled. Men
hopped and bellowed.

"Jezzus!"

"God's teeth!"

"Mother, Mary and Joseph!"

"Get a grip now, men." Someone barked out.
"Steady on. Get the girl, string her up on that tree."

"Wait." Veri smelled a horse near, heard its
harsh breaths, felt the thunk as it rose and landed,
rearing for certain. She peeked to see a man
dismounting. This one did not wear the protective
clothes of a warrior, but finely woven surcoats and a
tunic of fabric so smooth it didn't seem to be fabric at
all. There was no fear of his striking out with his feet,
covered in soft pliable leather. As though the earth's
shudders, its quaking, were no great thing, he passed
the reins of his agitated horse to another and crossed
to Veri. The only telltale sign the earth rumbled was
the way he walked, as one would cross the deck of a
swaying ship.

"What poison did you give him?" He asked. "What berries did you use?"

The other men fought to control horses, hid behind trees and bushes, as though being hidden would save them from the wildness of the land. Others tried to cram into the small hut with the man called Roland. But this man, this one man, remained steady and true.

The ground stilled, the chaos quieted.

"What?" He shook her by the shoulders, but not like the others had. His intent was not to hurt, but jog her into answering.

"Sleeping herbs. He will wake." Lips swollen beyond use, Veri was afraid he couldn't understand.

He leaned in, studied her face to face. "Sleeping draught?"

She nodded, not able to speak. He let her go. She fell to the ground, tears mixing with the blood on her face. She didn't know what happened next, she didn't care. Moment by moment, she assessed pain, ignored fear, for it would change nothing. Her hands were pulled behind her back and bound, as were her feet. Bruised and battered, she had no fight to offer. Even her trembling stopped as she gave way to resignation.

"You will hang," the steady one promised, "but not here, not without witness. You will hang where the whole of Oakland, and its people, can see you dangle."

There was no hope.

CHAPTER 6 ~ HOME AGAIN

Cocooned in feather bedding, Roland woke to the view of a silk canopy and curtains. Home, he was home, could have wept with the relief of it, except he was too sick to feel any relief. Sweat beaded against the spinning that caused his stomach to roil.

Still, he managed to whisper one word of gratitude to the child, Veri, who somehow managed to get him home. There had been no sickness before, when he was with the child. He was in her debt.

A rustle drew his head to the side, a costly error.

"You're awake, then?"

There had been no need to turn and look to see who was with him. No one else could speak with so little inflection. His stepmother, Hannah.

With great effort he tried to sit, to pull himself up against the pillows, but he proved no match to the revolt of his stomach. Hannah was there with a bowl, prepared, as he had not been. The retching pulled at his already tortured body, his head spun.

"They must have poisoned you." Hannah offered, no sympathy, no accusation. She dealt in facts or what were, to her, facts.

Roland could no more communicate than argue. There was little to heave, yet heave he did, with a furnace full of heat that quickly turned to chills. All the while his body writhed to expel whatever it wanted to purge.

He remembered now, the torture of sickness, when he had been well on the road to recovery. Now there was no comfort, despite a vague recollection of soothing words, gentle touches. Those would be from

Dori, sweet little Dori, his younger sister, trying to ease his pain. His other sister, Margaret, had been there too, issuing orders, not that orders could stop whatever was happening. It seemed to last forever before, exhausted and aching, he fell back into a restless sleep.

How long he slept, how long illness clawed at him, he could not tell, but he was well past missing the young child's care, past wishing for the numbness the child caused. Death would be welcome, if it would come for him.

"Roland?" Dori was back, with her kind voice, her gentle hand to his head. "Drink this, please."

That he could hear the pleading, the worry in her voice, told him more than he dared believe. The torture of sickness was fading. Carefully, he dared to look at her.

No shift, no stomach roiling whirl. Bowl in hand, Dori stood rock steady beside the bed.

"You are waking? Oh, please God, you are waking?"

Without waiting for an answer, she put the bowl to his lips but he refused it. Too many people had been giving him sips of this and that. He didn't doubt his suffering was due to such potions.

"It's merely water, Roland, nothing else." She promised. "You know herbs and such are not my strength. And I wouldn't hurt you with any trials."

"No." He agreed. Dori would never hurt him but he couldn't explain, for that took more stamina than he had.

"Please," she begged, misunderstanding his 'no,' putting the bowl to his mouth again with a determination that had it spilling down his chin. "Oh?" she fretted, but he was too thirsty to worry, just opened his mouth, prepared for manna to the desert of his mouth.

Water. Had no one thought of that before? Greedy for every drop she had, he moaned when she removed the vessel.

"Careful," Dori admonished, "little sips first."

As eager as his body had been to expel all that it held, it now wanted to fill itself. "More." He startled his younger sister. "More, please."

"There's a broth." She moved away from him, to the fire. "I brought it from the kitchens, but there are no herbs . . . I just don't know about such things. But Hannah is with father, he needs her. I just don't know what to do."

So it went through the night, Dori administering water and broth, neither speaking beyond a gentle touch from her, a grateful look from Roland, broken by short drifts to blissful unconsciousness.

A small semblance of strength returned when the first light cast its beam into the room, waking Roland to a Dori slumbering in a chair, her head upon his bedside. Grateful for even that meager advantage, he managed to raise his hand, to stroke her hair in gratitude for his sister, the young girl who had grown into such a treasure of a young lady.

Girl.

Girl? Yes! Jarred by his forgetfulness, his memory flooded. The girl, the child, who watched over him in a hut, who must have returned him to his home.

Dori, roused by his touch, looked up.

"The child, Veri, how did she get me here?" He asked, startled when Dori's gentle smile turned hard.

"Don't worry about the likes of her, brother dear. She will be well past this life by morning's end."

More emotion than ability shot Roland up, to sit, bewildered. "What? What do you speak of? She saved my life, Dori. She is not to die."

"She gave you a sleeping potion. You nearly died . . ." Her words dropped off as Roland shook his head and struggled to get free of the covers, to rise from the bed.

"No!" Alarmed, she tried to push him back, imprison him with the blankets he tried so hard to escape. "No! You do not rise yet. I will go, I will try to find her."

She turned to run, to do just as he asked when he grabbed her arm. "How long has it been, Dori? How long has she faced . . . " He couldn't go on, finish the thought, for he could not bear to think of her in the dungeon or worse.

Dori's hesitation heightened the fear that gripped him with more power than the illness had.

"Move, Dori!" He commanded. "I vowed to protect her."

"No." She tried to stop him again. "I will go and see what is about." She patted his chest to comfort, he supposed, though her confusion did not ease him. "I will go."

"Go swiftly, please Dori. I pledged to protect her. Go swiftly." And I will follow, he did not tell her, for she would not leave if she knew that.

When she hesitated he demanded. "Go, Dori! Run! Shout out to stop before any harm comes to her. Go!" He clambered from the bed as she disappeared through the doorway. "Dear God, go, and find her well."

CHAPTER 7 ~ THE DUNGEON

The smell of meaty stew, steeped in gravy reached her. Veri didn't eat meat, so the smell should not tempt, but tempt it did. Because it was food. Something she had not had for the days she had been locked within this cage, hovering above a room in a cave.

At least she thought it a cave, for it had no windows, no air other than the foul stench of men's bodies and rotting carcasses and the odor of waste. Human carcasses and waste. These were not clean people, it was not a tidy place. Dis-ease would have a merry hand here.

Veri shifted against the pain of the slats of her cage, not that it helped. There was no relief from the uneven pieces of wood that pressed against her legs, her back, whatever part of her tried to rest against them. No one had fed her, though they noticed her. It would be better if they didn't. They poked at her with long sticks. Offered her rags soaked in putrid water.

She had sucked on those, eager, greedy, for that was the only sustenance offered. Even as she forced it down, her throat tried to send it back, gagging with the texture, the taste.

She knew the damage to her body, broken rib, teeth loosened, one gone. The swelling in her lip and eye were still evident. She wondered if she would live long enough for them to heal.

Not that it mattered.

The knight called Roland had not come to show her the wonders of this place called Oakland, to have her dressed in fine fabrics and fancy jewels. He did not tell her about this place of cruelty, where men were chained to the walls until they grew so thin their hands slipped from the manacles.

It was a place of moans and groans and screams. There was no knowing day from night. That was not unusual for her, living in caves. But in the caves there had been routine. Until now, Veri had not known how the order gave way to succession in the day. She knew, by what needed to be done, whether the sky would be bright or dark, should she go outside.

Here, without even meals to assess the changes, the only way she could know if merely one long day had passed or a whole phase of the moon was by the strength of her hunger. It was more than a day but, she doubted, less than one Sabbath to another.

Hunger and pain had become her, taken her over, so she knew no different, was edging past the point of hoping for some other way to feel.

A key rattled in the lock. The keeper, a burly man, stood quickly, leaving his meal to steam upon a table. His rodent eyes scanned the area, searching for fault. Curled into a ball in the corner of her cage, Veri didn't dare move, lest her cage, hanging from rafters as it was, would swing and bring attention her way.

Voices echoed off the walls. Visitors or a new victim of this room with its racks and torturous devices, she didn't know, couldn't tell, but knew that the other prisoners, men chained to walls, pushed into cells smaller than her little cage, all noticed. None dared cry out for fear of retribution, but there was a sudden stillness tinged with hope, balanced by dread.

Discomfited as his prisoners, the beefy keeper tugged on his braes, adjusted the vest he wore that failed to cover his rotund belly.

People were coming down the steps.

"You've not fed her?" She remembered that voice from the attack. The steady one, the one dressed in fine clothes. He promised she would hang.

A ripple of relief, palpable, eased the other prisoners, as they realized the visitors came for Veri, not them.

"No, m'lord." The keeper could see them first, answered the question, all meek and groveling when usually he was mean and sour- tempered. His brutality would return with interest after the visitors left, as though his cowardice had to be countered by cruelty. "She's starved so she don't even drop her shit through the cage no more."

Past the humiliation of her predicament, Veri didn't care what was said, only feared what they might do. She breathed deep, told herself 'this is a learning' and pulled even further into herself. Willed herself to be so small, she could drop through the holes of the cage and disappear in the soiled reeds below.

She was not successful.

She hid behind her closed eyes, as though others couldn't see her if she didn't see them. Clenched in tight, breath held, she waited. So many voices when others rarely entered this place and a woman, different to the one who had come before. That one stood and stared at Veri, her nose flaring like an animal catching the scent.

It was a bad place to catch scents.

"Just outside the gate." A deep voice explained. "They've built a frame. Let her be a lesson to them all!"

"Vultures will pick her bones if they can get into her."

"Let the sun fry her."

"Let her starve as she robbed him of sustenance."

Robbed who? She kept no one from food. Worked hard to care for the man called Roland, went out to gather foods for his broth.

How had she robbed him of sustenance?

"Witch!"

There was that word again. "Witch" spit out like the vilest of sounds.

She was a healer, bound to caring for others, set upon easing life, saving life, not doing harm.

The cage swung wildly. Veri opened her eyes, as she grabbed the slats to steady herself just as her world veered sharply to the right, then dropped to the ground. She bounced with it, lost her grip, flung from top to bottom, side to side, jolting an already aching body.

"She's just a child." A woman cried.

"A child who fed your brother poison just to steal a measly bag." It was the skinny man, with the leather jerkin, who had captured her by the coal maker's hut.

"Sir Robert!" Her voice rang with authority, quelling dissension and with it, offering the first glimpse of hope. Veri was well- accustomed to strong, intelligent women. Trusted in the power and will of such women. Surely this one would see her innocence and set her free.

But the woman startled rather than calmed. Used to the simple garb of peasants and town-folk, Veri thought to averted her gaze but could not. The woman's deep blue bliaut fit so close it outlined her female shape. The side of the trumpet sleeve opened in three wide slashes revealing a yellow chemise bright as a field of rapeseed, and so tight it had to have been sewn on.

Even hunger could not stave off fascination of so much color within the filth of a dungeon. It promised outdoors, sunlight and blue skies. Veri tried to reach out, as though mere touch could transform her, send her outside. She sighed, on the verge of tears, so certain that this woman, in her fine colored clothes, trimmed with threads of gold and sparkling green gems, was here to change all, just as her appearance changed all within this space.

The grand lady shook her head, ever so slightly, but it could not be mistaken, for the linen head covering, so fine you could see through it, quivered with the movement.

No longer wary, Veri watched, entranced, so trusting in feminine power to do right, to be kind and just, relief burgeoned.

Gentle, yet firm, the woman spoke. "She is a child. Surely there was some caretaker who directed her. Have you spoken to her? Have you asked her what she gave to Roland to make him so ill? Have you asked who her parents are? Have you looked to the villagers to see what they know of her?"

"Aye, Lady Margret," the keeper bowed to this woman. "that's what I do, I get answers."

The woman stepped down the last stair and away from him, as if he were as filthy as the place, which he was and Veri whimpered, not meaning to, but hope was such a scary thing.

And then the steady man came forward, taking the woman by the arm. "This is no place for you, Margret. Let me take you upstairs."

"No, Lord William." Lady Mercy, for that is how Veri saw her, not Margret but Mercy. "Bigge may have asked her, but I do not think he knows how to gentle a horse, let alone reveal the truth of a child. I will ask questions myself."

"She is not so different from an animal." Someone mumbled, but Veri didn't care who, didn't care to look anywhere but at this woman with her peculiar clothes and gentle voice. The Lady moved toward her, as though she floated over the filthy rushes.

"Do you have a name, child?"

Veri shot a glance at Bigge and then at the other men standing around. That had been one of their questions before. When she had answered, they had poked sharp spears into her cage.

"Come child, surely you have a name."

Cautious, Veri held back, as another woman came forward, the one who had come and stared without saying anything.

This woman had the same under garment and over garment but these were of plain cloth, no colors, no gold or sparkling gems and not pulled so tight. Dual natures, as different as their clothes, Veri did not doubt. Lady Margaret, although frowning, had a softness to her. This other woman did not. She was strong and severe. Tansy could be severe.

But these were women, not like men.

She would answer and hope that they would free her from the men.

"Veri." She whispered.

"See!" Bigge shouted. "Have you ever heard anyone called such a name?"

"And your people, Veri?" The hard woman asked.

Again, Veri watched the men shift, uncomfortable it seemed, at having their plans slowed.

This was a learning, she had to remember that. Later, she might understand why tears came to her when this was, possibly, her best moment since being taken from her home. This was the first moment anyone really listened.

"Please, the sisters at Our Lady's know of me." If possible, tears would pool and stream, though there were none, as she had so little water within her. They were dry tears that hurt her eyes with the hope that mayhap, these fine ladies would send for Rose or Edith or any of the others.

She had been so alone.

The one called Lady Margaret straightened. The other woman looked closer, studied each of Veri's features, her ragged hair, before pulling back hard, hatred in her eyes. Abhorrence, for a moment only, then nothing. Blank.

Danger.

She finally spoke. "Do not hang her in the cage. Hang her by the neck, to dangle in death for all to see." As quickly as she spoke, she turned, walked through the crowd to the stairs.

"Hannah," Lady Margaret argued, "she is familiar with the women at the convent. Surely, with your Christian heart, you will at least wait to see what they have to say."

"Hang her." Hannah said, to no one as she started up the steep stone steps. "You can't believe that she is convent bound. Look at the raggedy thing. She is no more than a scavenger herself. So leave her to the vultures. To her own."

"I will not have it." Lady Margaret argued.

Halfway up the stairs, Hannah stopped, looked down at Lady Margaret. "You are not mistress here."

"No, mayhap not." Margaret agreed, "But both my father and Roland are still breathing. The fate of this child is not for you to decide."

"Your father wants the girl to suffer as his son has. As for Sir Roland, he will be dead within a day himself."

"No, no, no, no, no." Past caution, Veri mumbled the impossibility of it, as she curled into a ball in the far corner of the cage.

Dead? Within a day? He was healing when she last saw him. What was this monstrous place. How could this happen? She had worked so hard to make him better. He never suffered in her care.

She yelped, scrambled from her corner. Bigge's gnarled teeth showed as he smiled, prodding a pointed stick through the slats. Veri dodged, but the space was small and the point sharp. Little slashes and pricks welled with blood.

Lady Margaret reached out, grabbed the pole by its center, spearing Bigge with a look as sharp as the pike. "Desist. Roland is not dead," she looked at Hannah, "yet, anyway. Is he?"

Hannah's response was a haughty sniff, but the offense was on her, for the stench of the place had her putting a kerchief to her nose. "It matters not. Lord Hugh wants her hung. Today. This very morning. See to it." She pointed to the household guardsmen standing behind the others. "There is no time to waste. She is the devil's spawn. Let him see how we treat those who do his bidding."

Hugging the wall, a maid came down the stairs, lent down and whispered to Hannah.

"Speak up, girl." Hannah snapped.

"Lady Doreena is looking for you."

"Ah," she looked to Margaret. "Dori was with Roland. Shall we see what she has to say?"

Hannah climbed the stairs. Sir William moved closer to Lady Margaret, urged her aside, as soldiers surrounded the cage, slid poles through the upper slats to act as carrier braces.

"You know she will have her way in the end, Margaret.' He told her, "You are only prolonging your distress."

"There has been too much sorrow in this household. I will not have Roland a victim, too."

Sir William nodded. "No."

"And this child here is not to fault for all our pain. I will not have her blamed when we should be finding who is to fault."

"Margaret," William argued, "I was there. He said she would pay for what she had done. He said first his brothers and now this. Roland himself spoke of her guilt."

"Roland must not die!" Sorrow welled in her words, as she looked to Veri. "What did you give him? What have you done?"

"No poison." Veri promised, hoping this one woman could save her. "A sleeping potion. That was all." The cage shook, as soldiers lifted the poles to their shoulders, heading for the wide stairs. "Just a sleeping draught so he would rest." She reached through the bars for Margaret, earning a swat of the whip from Bigge.

She rubbed her arms. "He would not rest, so I gave him a sleep potion. He needed to rest."

Sir William turned Margaret away. "The child stole his leather pouch. Who knows what else she managed to take earlier. She is a liar and a thief."

"She is just a child. I do not want to see a child hang."

"Then do not watch, Margaret. Go to your rooms, rest. It will be over quickly."

Clinging to the cage, her face pressed to the slats, Veri watched Margaret's back, willing her to turn around, to listen . . . to save her.

Instead, Margaret turned into Sir William's hold, burying her face, hiding from a fate she could not change.

CHAPTER 8 ~ THE GALLOWS

Roland's head lifted, though he lacked the strength to get up and look. No need to look, he could hear the crowd gathered below, in the courtyard. A rowdy crowd.

"Do they gather for my death?" His father whispered from the cocoon of his bed.

They were a pair, the two of them. Roland, weak as his worst nightmare, had rousted a page to help him dress and get to his father's bedside. His powerful, invincible father, Lord Hugh, who now had barely the strength to breathe.

Roland sent the page to find his little healer. She would know what to do, if there was anything that could be done. Until she was there, he would hold hope.

"You are not dead, father. Once we have young Veri here, to nurse you, you will be gaining in strength." This earned a meager nod, in resignation or belief, Roland couldn't tell.

So much mourning. Between the attack and healing, there was no time to think of his brothers. Now, sitting by his father's bed, looking at the shrunken man, afraid he might lose him, their absence proved a keen wound.

He was certain the child, Veri, would be well. If that were not the case, Dori would have informed him by now. Where was she and where was Ulric? Both should have brought word by now if something drastic threatened. If Veri were in some sort of danger.

Dori could be bathing the girl, tending to her, making her comfortable, presentable. Ulric was probably still looking for her.

The crowd grew louder.

"Shall I read to you, father?" Thinking to distract them both.

His father waved a skeleton- thin hand toward the windows, then dropped it to the bed.

"The ruckus? You want to know what it is?"

Roland pushed up from the chair. With a hand to the bed post, he steadied himself, realized he was gaining some stamina. He could walk to the window.

The page, Ulric, rushed into the room as Roland reached the opening overlooking the courtyard, the noise growing louder, clearer and froze as Ulric stammered, "They mean to hang her! They are taking her . . ."

As quickly as he stilled, Roland moved into action, horror over-riding limitation.

"Get me down there, now!" He shouted, panicked by what he saw.

Roland took a step and faltered. Ulric caught him, lifted Roland's arm over his shoulder, and the two headed for the stairs, Roland gaining strength with each step. By the time they reached the stairs, they were taking two at a time, until Roland had to stop. "Go ahead, get a horse, any horse, steal one!"

He leaned against the wall of the stairwell, breathing quickly. Until he pictured, once again, Veri in a cage, being hauled to the gallows. Galvanized, he reached the entry, three stories high, empty, everyone having run outside to see to the hanging.

The walls were lined with swords and hatchets, pikes and shields, all manner of weapon. All too high to reach without aide, to heavy to lift when one could barely hold himself upright.

Even through the solid wood doors he heard the commotion. Shouting, yelling and horses.

Ulric would have found a horse.

Roland reached the portal. Pushed at the oak barrier with every last ounce of strength. There was a smaller, man- sized door, but Roland needed the large, ceremonial opening. The keep was in good order, the hinges well- oiled, he managed the opening, spied Ulric below and signaled.

He refused to look to the gallows, didn't listen to the jeers and cheering, knowing what they meant. There was little time, no time. He didn't care. He would succeed. He would help her and God save anything that tried to make him think differently.

* * * * * * * * * *

On all fours in the cage, white knuckled to keep from falling with the sway, Veri kept her head down. There was no use dodging the refuse thrown at her. There was nowhere to dodge to.

She had never cried like this before, silent streams of tears, whimpers of shame. What had she done, who had she hurt?

"Witch, witch, witch!" Everyone was chanting, calling out.

She was not a witch. They had it all wrong. She was a healer. That was all. That was good. That was the best that she was. A healer.

"Devil's spawn!"

She crouched down as close to the bottom of the cage as she could, curled, thinking furiously of how to free herself from this place, these people. Words had not helped her even though she lied. Tansy had taught her what to say and she did. She told them she was an orphan, child of a traveling coal maker and his wife. They had died, she was alone, trying to get to the Sisters at Our Lady's.

No one would listen. No one wanted to hear.

She had not told them she was a healer. They should not be calling her witch.

They had stopped, but she was afraid to look and risk animal waste in her face. There was already too much thrown, unmistakable by its smell. She tried to peek, but all she could see was a cart and the back of a horse.

Perhaps they were going to send her away. That would be ok. She would go get Tansy, then go to the convent. She wouldn't let Tansy argue. These people did not deserve to be helped. They were angry and cruel.

They started moving again, the soldiers carrying her dividing to either side of the cart.

"Hang her, hang her, hang her!" Everyone shouted together, the words waving through the crowd.

Veri steadied as the cage was loaded onto the cart. She wondered where they would hang it, as the people kept calling for them to do so.

Bigge swaggered toward her, his legs wide-spread, his shoulders back. No more cowering for Bigge. He held a key. The key to let her out? The key to free her?

He put it in the lock, clicked it free. With a creak of the hinge, the door swung open.

She should scurry out, run for freedom, she should rejoice.

She didn't trust him. Crouched, a wary animal anticipating an unfair chase, she hovered in her place.

"Out with you!" he bellowed.

Still, she hesitated.

"Out!" He reached in, grabbed and yanked her out. "I told you to move."

Raw sores grazed against the willow as she fought against the dragging, tried to gain purchase with her toes, to find her own way out. He still had her arm, when she broke free, stood for the first time. Muscles now accustomed to squatting refused to hold her. She crumpled.

'Up on top of the basket."

Veri spun to see the lady called Hannah standing by the cart. She had a big book in her hand.

"Try to be a good girl," Hannah said. "Get on top of the basket. Perhaps God will reward you for obedience."

Freedom was the only reward she wanted. If the cage was to be her seat for the ride to that end, she would comply. She leveraged herself on top of the small prison, now on that wide, flat- bed cart. There were no sides and only two wheels. Soldiers braced it at each corner. Two more stood on boxes on either side of the cage, within a stone arch, an entrance through the inner castle wall.

One of the soldiers grabbed her arms, forcing them behind her, yanking hard when she tried to turn, to see what he was doing. He whipped a rope around her wrists, pulled tight to secure it. Too tight, the blood would stop running to her fingers. She tried, without luck, to flex her wrists.

Something hit her in the shoulder, so she craned, saw a loop of rope dangling beside her, and traced it to the other end. It went up and over a cross beam of the raised gate, then over to an iron loop in the wall, where it was fastened.

The soldier standing in front of her grabbed the loop and lobbed it over her head before she took a breath. With a yank, he made it fit close to her neck.

She didn't understand. Was this another way to manacle a person?

The two who had bound her jumped from the cart, making it sway and tilt precariously. Veri used her toes to stay steady, ride it.

Silence. Everyone had been so loud, busy throwing things, being hateful. Now that she would be leaving, they quieted.

This was a strange place but she didn't care because soon, she would be gone.

She waited, wondering when they would cut the rope where it was attached to the arch wall, for she couldn't go forward until then.

A drum roll played, an odd thing to fill the silence. But she was going home. She would soon be safe. She relaxed as she looked at all the people looking at her. They seemed on the edge something huge; something far bigger than a young girl going home.

The soldiers balancing the cart let go, two more gripped the cage, when suddenly another slapped the rump of the horse.

"Nooooo," Veri started to rail, knowing, by the weight of it, the rope was still attached to the wall. But there was no time for a keen cry; the horse bolted, the cage was pulled from beneath her and Veri felt herself fall, fall, fall to be jerked by the neck, no longer able to feel anything, to see anything but blackness.

* * * * * * * * *

Without question, Ulric responded to Roland's gesture and brought the horse straight up the stairs. To that, he'd chosen the right horse as well. A useful lad when times were difficult.

"Help me." A request that should have meant full body armor, or some equal detriment. Roland didn't care, pride was not part of this. He was just grateful that the lad was as strong as he was smart.

"Open the door wider." Roland nodded to where he left the huge portal ajar, Ulric pulled both wings wide of the entrance.

"Now go, shouting as you do! Stop them, before it's too late. I will follow." Roland commanded.

Upon the horse, in the keep, Roland heard Ulric shouting at the top of his voice, "Halt this! I tell you halt! Sir Roland said to stop!"

By horseback, Roland could reach a cross bow and the arrows in a quiver beside it. Once in hand, he loaded the bow, turned the horse, crossed the portal and made his way down the stairs.

"Make way or be trampled. Make way."

A sea of people pushed and pulled, grabbing children from his path, as an eerie quiet descended. Too quiet.

Roland looked up, a cry billowing though sound would not help him here. It all slowed, each minute movement caught. Ulric fought against the crowd. All around the fight others stared at the child on the crate, the noose, the rope. A soldier lift his hand to swat the cart horse, a collective gasp ballooned in the air. He lifted the bow as the cart horse bunched its muscles to bolt,as the house guard reached, to pull the cage from beneath Veri.

From nowhere, wind, hot, scouring like the sand devils of the desert, blast across the courtyard.

Breath held tight, eyes narrowed against the sting of debris, he aimed. The depth of a blade of grass his only buffer between life, death. A moving target, relaxed coil of rope, lifting, tightening as the arrow flew from the bow, over the heads of the crowd, past the fleeing cart horse, skimming over the man holding the cage. The arrow point touched the tautening rope, split it, just as Ulric reached the girl. He caught her as she fell, unconscious, toward the ground.

The strange wind stopped.

Silence descended. A strange and eerie ending for a hanging. No shouts of hoorah. No cheers. Instead they all looked to Roland, upon his horse, a sorry sight, for he was starved of air. No matter how much he dragged in, he could not get enough.

That did not stop him. A kick to Spirit's sides, he urged him forward, toward Ulric, whose horror mirrored the crowd's.

What had they done?

A surge of power had him reaching Veri, dismounting, pulling her onto his lap, as all that power withered. An invalid again, in need of his little healer for, once again, he had overshot his own abilities.

"She was to be my guest." He mumbled, "My honored guest."

Bowed over her, his numbness gave way to tears for the loss of his brothers, the failing of his father and now the death of a sweet child who had saved his life.

"Please don't die." He whispered. "Please don't die, I promise I will protect you." He rocked as he sat, rocked the child as a mother would rock a fretful babe. He rocked to the rhythm of sorrow.

She coughed, choked. He nearly dropped her in surprise, but caught her back to him.

"Veri?" Her eyes flutter. "You live." Still whispering. The crowd pressed in, he gestured them away. "Give her space, room to breathe."

Her eyes opened. She looked up at him.

"I'm sorry, little one." He brushed a strand of hair from her forehead. "I am sorry. But I will make it up to you, I promise. You will never have to fear again." He pulled her up, held her close to his chest. "Nothing to fear, ever again. I will protect you."

He trusted she felt safe, for she slipped into a sleep that would hold her close for near on three days. Three days before he could give her his name, the protection of his family, a home at Oakland Castle.

Three days before she would awaken and tend to his father, bringing him back to health. Three days before the rest of their lives; husband and wife in name, secure within a family, smaller now, but with it the wealth and stature as Lady of Oakland Castle.

And with his father's health, he would go on crusade with the promise she would be there upon his return, grown to a fine young lady. Then, when he returned and she had grown, they would become one in body, as well as soul, the Montgomery family would blossom with the birth of the their children.

His Veri.

Alive and safe beneath his protection.

Hope you have enjoyed this prequel to THE PROTECTOR

EXCERPT ~ THE PROTECTOR
PROLOGUE ~ IN THE YEAR OF OUR LORD 1226

"Do you think he means to find her?"

"If it be true, I pray the Lord he fails."

"He ne'er fails," an old voice prophesied from deep within the corner.

Shadows danced upon the kitchen walls as three young serving maids abandoned their sleeping pallets to huddle closer together within the kitchen.

"Gelda, is that you?" Maida, the oldest of the girls, asked.

"Aye, 'tis me." Bow-backed and wobbly, Gelda moved into the light from the dying fire, her cane tapping the floor with each shuffled step. "And true as my word, he will find her. He will find her and bring her back here to burn for her sins."

"'Tis true then?" Maida's best friend Bertha, whispered in fear. "She truly bewitched all the men in the castle?"

"Every one of them!" Gelda announced. "And finally, Sir Roland is back to hear the full of it, to hear how his men would gather for wild nights of wantonness. That his wife would have them all, bewitched every one of them!"

"The knights speak naught of this!" Cwen, the youngest, stated boldly.

Gelda's eyes glinted in the firelight. "Do you think a mighty warrior wants to brag of a witch's spell over him? Besides, there are others for the telling, others who have seen."

Maida and Bertha shook their heads in answer before Maida hissed, "She poisoned his father, then drank of the poison herself. My auntie told me."

"Aye," Gelda affirmed, "But she did not die of the foul brew. 'Tis testament to her witchery."

Cwen stepped toward Gelda, as if no shadow could cast fear her way. "My mum told me his lordship's wife is no witch. 'Twas her who saved his lordship's life and the life of his father."

"Nay," chorused the other girls, "she's a witch, to be sure. How else did she escape the room where she was held?"

Gelda watched young Cwen closely, but the child held her ground, flinching only when the old hag lifted her cane to point toward her courageous stance.

"Aye, she is a witch. 'Tis well known that witches are shape shifters, that they be cat or bird or any number of beasts as easily as they be women. That's what she did, she did. She shifted herself into a huge bird, to fly from the window."

Bertha squeaked in fear. "My father saw such a thing once, when he went to the woods with Father Ignacious."

Gelda moved back, blending into the darkness, thinking her mistress would be well pleased with this night. Fear grew like the mustard seed, easily fed, easily spread. Standing silently, nodding, Gelda listened as the disquiet she had so artfully planted, ripened.

"They'd gone to burn the witches of the woods." All eyes were upon the teller of the tale, "But the witches brought the hail down."

"Aye, that's the truth, my granny told me of that day. The crops were heavy, ready to harvest. They were ruined. 'Tis true!"

"'Tis that, indeed. And after they brought the hail they turned into a flock of crows, flying away, just as easily as you please, escaping the wrath of God and his vengeance."

"God will get them one day, he will."

"And God alone knows the truth of it!" Cwen scorned, "My mum told me Lady Veri is no witch."

"That's 'cuz your mum was bewitched by her. T'would be easily done, as she was her maid when Lord Roland brought her home with him."

"M' mum was no prisoner of witches!"

"Shhh," Gelda hissed, "lest you wake those out in the hall."

The fire popped and hissed. Bertha and Maida darted into each other's arms, trembling with fear. Even Cwen pulled her robe tighter about her, as she looked to the darkened corners of the kitchen.

"'Tis time you sleep," the old woman admonished, "'twill be a long day on the morrow, what with his Lordship just back from the holy wars."

"Who could sleep for fear she might come to take him?"

"She wouldn't be doing that. She'll stay clear of Oakland Castle." Maida assured, confidently.

Bertha shook her head, "I'll be praying he doesn't find her. I'll be praying mightily."

"Pray all you want, but that won't stop him from finding her and seeking vengeance."

"What if she were to kill him and eat him first?"

"Witches don't eat grown men." Maida snorted, "They eat children."

"Nooooo," Bertha wailed.

"They eat children for sure, but she'll not be coming here. Father Ignacious blessed this house once she was gone. She'll melt to a puddle should she try to return."

Round-eyed Bertha stared. "What do you think she looks like now?"

"No one knows for a surety." Maida whispered, knowingly. "Witches can look anyway they please, but I heard that Taylor's son once saw her as an eagle. So, 'tis not a worry. Even if his lordship were to find her, he'd never be able to catch her. She'd just fly away. 'Tis how it's done."

Heads came together, two in consultation, one with cautious curiosity, as Maida continued, "Come All Hallows Eve we'll see her shadow against the full moon. That's the time to worry. But not now. Not when Lord Roland is home. He's a mighty warrior who fought for the Jesus. He had God on his side. He will slay her just like he slayed the infidels."